I0766461

Golden Tails

Written by Taylor Maiman and Sara Buske

Illustrated by Joanna Becker

Illustrated by Joanna Becker

Dedicated to Addie

We hope for all the best things
in life for you & may you share
in our love of reading, travel, and dogs.

Love,

Mommy & Mimi

Today is a very exciting day for me. It's the day I meet and go home with my new family.

I hope my family likes me! I am a bit nervous...
I'm still learning when to go potty.

Should I go in the car? Am I allowed to go in the parking lot?
I'm not sure where to go and I want to be a good boy.

Oh Boy! My family has arrived! It's time to go to my new home!
EEK!

The car ride was very interesting. I loved looking out the window at all the sights.

I must have been too excited because I felt something warm and wet where I was sitting.
I piddled right there in the car! It was so embarrassing.

I know my new family has another dog. She is a little older than me.
Her name is Maya and I cannot wait to meet and learn new things from her.

Finally, we pulled up to my new house and I saw Maya in the window and *everyone* said:
"Welcome home, Carson!"

My tail wagged like a helicopter. I leaped out of the car smelling everything around me.

Then I saw Maya coming to greet me.

I felt a bit shy and slowly wiggled over to Maya.
Something warm and wet dribbled out.

Oh no, I piddled again!

I didn't want to disappoint my new family but they were very understanding. They picked me up and sat me on the grass to finish my business.

Maya came to me and said, "Carson, let me show you around".
We explored my new yard and it was HUGE.

We could run from one side of the fence to the other!

We went inside the house to see my new home.

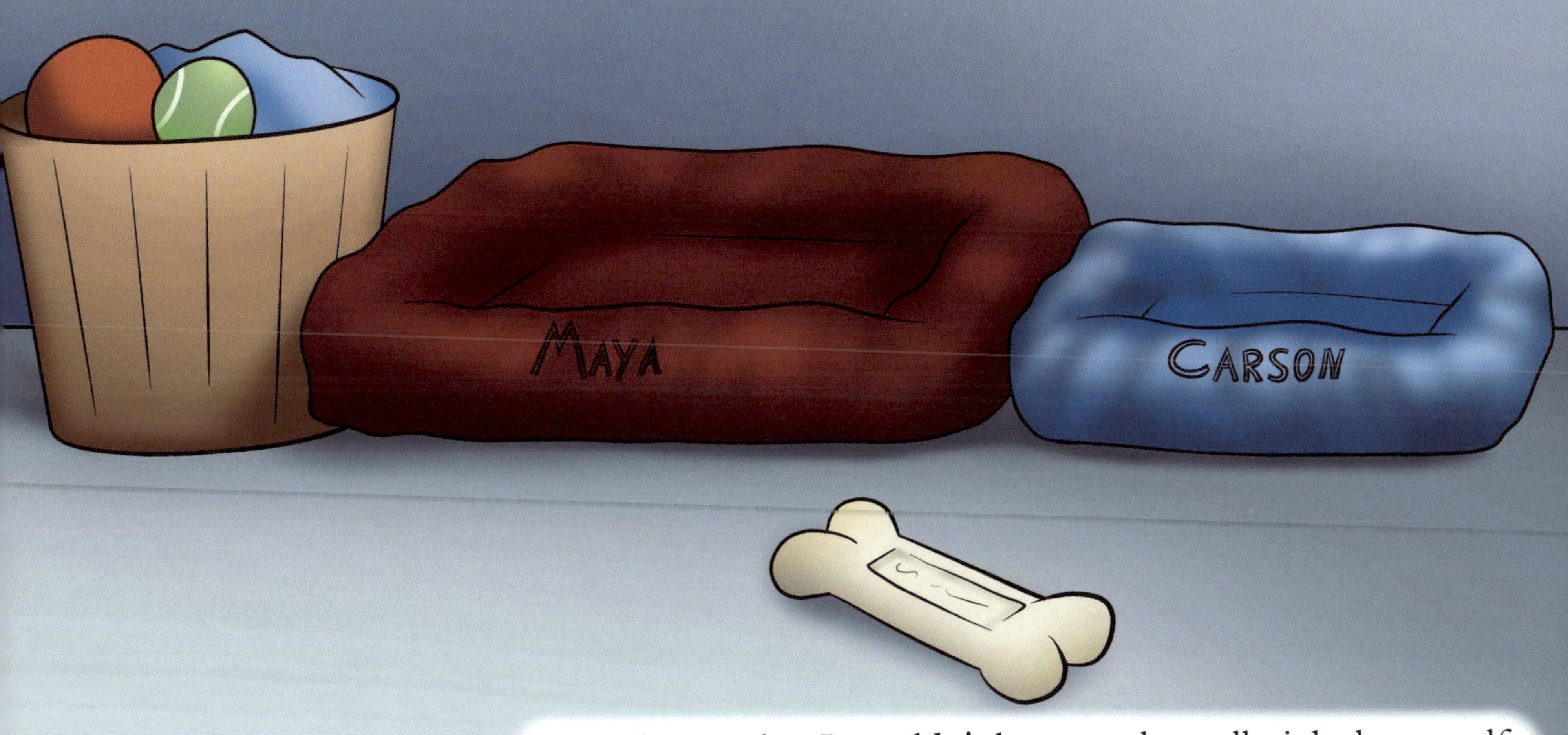

There were toys for Maya and me to share. I had a new bed of my own to sleep and take naps in. Maya's bed was near mine.

I was happy that I wouldn't have to sleep all night by myself.

Someone yelled:

"CARSON, MAYA, TIME FOR DINNER!"

When I saw Maya run for the kitchen I chased after her sliding into a wall because I couldn't slow down fast enough!

I gulped my dinner down, it was SO GOOD!

After I ate my food I wandered and sniffed around the floor. I felt the urge to go potty and didn't know where I should go.

I found a corner and squatted. "No, no Carson, not again!" said Maya.

Maya led me by the collar to the backyard where she showed me the places where I should and shouldn't go potty.

"Not in the house, not in the car, and not in your bed," she told me.
Maya
Carson

"Carson, I had accidents in the beginning, too. Most of us do, that's why it's called potty training." Maya said, making me feel much better.

"Yea kid, Maya is right." I heard a deep voice say. I looked over at the fence and there was Rex, Maya's friend from next door.

Maya said, "Rex helped me learn where to go potty when I moved in."

Rex was quite nice and greeted me, "Welcome to the neighborhood, Carson. I'm not real fast anymore. But I helped Maya learn the rules around here. I'm happy to help you too, boy."

"Thanks Rex, it's nice to meet you." I barked.
"Don't worry, Carson," he said. "We'll make learning fun."

I couldn't help but jump in circles and chase my tail. I was SO happy.

It started to get late, and I was getting sleepy...
I told Maya, "I am worried I might have an accident tonight."

She said, "We'll go potty one more time before bed but no more water for you until morning. You've got this, Carson!"

Before long I wasn't having accidents and I was loving my new home. I love Maya and Rex.
MAYA
CARSON
They are such great friends and they're so good at teaching me that I don't have anything to worry about anymore. Everything comes out okay in the end.

The End

Maya (Left) & Carson (Right)

About the Authors:

Lifelong dog lovers Taylor and her stepmother Sara, along with their husbands, got Carson and Maya at the beginning of the Covid-19 pandemic in 2020. Carson and Maya are real life brother-sister litter mates from Salida, Colorado.

Sara lives in Edwardsville, Illinois with Taylor's father Tom, Maya, and 13 year old Rex. With the kids all grown they got the idea that Rex needed a new 'sister'.

After graduating in 2012 from the University of Colorado, Boulder, Taylor moved full-time to Denver, Colorado. She now resides in Arvada with her husband Kyle, their daughter Addison, and Carson.

Carson and Maya still see each other a couple of times a year. They love to play with each other and enjoy their adventures.

A special thank you to Ally and Andrew for their research & introducing us to such a responsible breeder, Kathy Armstrong owner of Moonlight Goldens.

9 781647 046026